The Little Wing Giver

Jacques Taravant

translated from the French by Nina Ignatowicz

illustrated by Peter Sís

Henry Holt and Company

New York

A *long, long time ago* when God had just created the world and when birds and bugs and butterflies didn't have wings, there lived a little boy. His nose was as round as a marble, and his cheeks softer than rose petals. His curly hair was black as night, and his eyes were bright as stars.

He traveled over mountains and fields, through forests and meadows, and along every road and stream singing this song:

Come get your wings.
Beautiful wings!
Come get your wings
And fly, fly, fly!

No one knew the little boy's name or where he came from. Perhaps he was born inside a flower one morning. Or perhaps he slid down to earth on a moonbeam one summer night. Or perhaps God had realized He'd forgotten to give out wings and sent the little boy to complete His creation.

What *is* important is that the little boy had a basket that was never empty, just like Santa Claus' bag. But the little boy's basket was not filled with toys. It was filled with every kind of wing imaginable—scissor-pointed wings for swallows, fluffy white wings for doves, gossamer wings for gnats, wooden wings for windmills.

The little boy gave wings to anyone who wanted them—eagles and humming-birds, ladybugs and vultures, parrots and sparrows. And as he walked along with his basket full of wings, he sang his song.

Come get your wings.
Beautiful wings!
Come get your wings
And fly, fly, fly!

Even though Little Wing Giver never asked for anything in return, the grateful nightingale sang him a pretty melody. The stork carried him on an exciting journey up into the clouds. The sparrow, who didn't know how to sing, thanked him by tilting its head to the side and bobbing it up and down. The bullfinch winked at him.

The owl hooted, "Whooo! Whooo!"
The ladybug made him laugh by gently
landing on the tip of his nose and tickling
it with her tiny feet—then *ffftt,* and she was
gone.

The parrot, who *did* know how to talk, said, "Thank you, they're just right!" The fly buzzed happily around Little Wing Giver before flying away. The blackbird whistled. And the pigeon, puffed up with pride because he could now show off his wings to the ladies, cooed his thanks.

Soon all the creatures you can think of had the wings they now have.

But as time passed, Little Wing Giver was getting more and more tired. One night, when he carefully put down his basket at the foot of an oak tree, and lay down to rest, a big storm rolled in. The wind, jealous of all the wings the little boy had given out, seized the basket and hurled all the wings into the ocean. Since that day, the ocean is filled with rushing waves—they are the wings trying in vain to rise out of the water and fly away.

When Little Wing Giver woke up the next morning and saw his basket gone, his heart was filled with sorrow. For a long, long time he wandered around, thinking of all the creatures he would never be able to help. At last he stopped in a meadow covered with poppies.

A small black caterpillar looked at Little Wing Giver and was so touched by his unhappiness, she tried to comfort him.

"Don't be sad," said the caterpillar. "Don't think about the wings you lost. Think of all the wings you gave! Think of all the birds and insects who can now fly because of you. Please don't cry. Look how hairy and ugly *I* am, yet I'm not crying!"

"How kind you are, caterpillar," Little Wing Giver answered. "Oh, how I wish I had a pair of wings to give you! Beautiful wings, wings as beautiful as a flower."

Suddenly, one of the poppies who had been listening whispered to Little Wing Giver.

"Pick me, little boy," she said. "Take my petals. They will make perfect wings for the caterpillar."

Little Wing Giver began to smile. Gently, he plucked off the poppy's petals and attached them to the caterpillar's back. And the caterpillar, now a beautiful butterfly, fluttered its wings in thanks and flew off.

That very evening Little Wing Giver lay down beside a brook and fell into a deep, deep sleep. Thousands of birds and butterflies and dragonflies gathered around him in the morning, waiting for their friend to open his eyes. The nightingale sang, the blackbird whistled, the parrot called to him, the ladybug tickled his little round nose with her feet.

As hard as they tried, they could not wake Little Wing Giver.

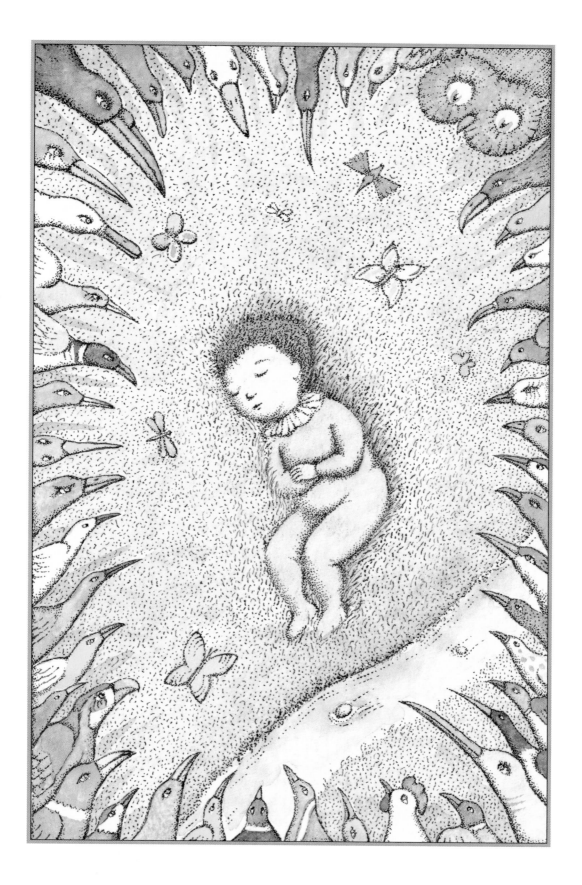

It's only by chance that a nosy magpie found two tiny dove wings forgotten in Little Wing Giver's pocket. Quickly, the birds attached the beautiful white wings to the sleeping boy's back. Then they stood back and watched as, with a graceful flap of his new wings, Little Wing Giver soared up into the sky.

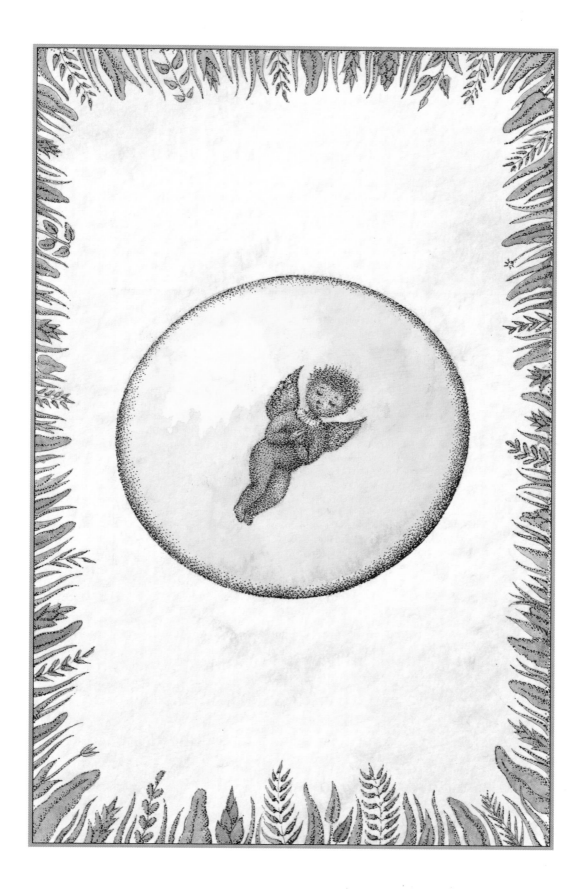

And it was on seeing Little Wing
Giver flying toward Him through a sunlit
cloud that gave God the idea of creating
angels.

For Jean-Marien

Henry Holt and Company, LLC, *Publishers since 1866*
115 West 18th Street, New York, New York 10011
Henry Holt is a registered trademark of Henry Holt and Company, LLC

Text copyright © 1997 by Bruno Taravant
Illustrations copyright © 1997 by Peter Sís
Translation copyright © 2001 by Henry Holt and Company
All rights reserved.
First published in the United States in 2001 by Henry Holt and Company, LLC.
Published in Canada by Fitzhenry & Whiteside Ltd., 195 Allstate Parkway, Markham, Ontario L3R 4T8.
Originally published in France in 1997 by Editions Grasset & Fasquelle under the title *Le marchand d'ailes.*

Library of Congress Cataloging-in-Publication Data
Taravant, Jacques.
[Marchand d'ailes. French]
The little wing giver / Jacques Taravant; translated by Nina Ignatowicz; illustrated by Peter Sís.
Summary: After giving wings to eagles, owls, nightingales, pigeons, ladybugs,
and all sorts of creatures, a small boy is given an appropriate reward.
[1. Wings—Fiction.] I. Sís, Peter, ill. II. Ignatowicz, Nina. III. Title.
PZ7.T1652Li 2001 [E]—dc21 00-47132

ISBN 0-8050-6412-5
First American Edition—2001 / Designed by Martha Rago
Printed in the United States of America on acid-free paper. ∞
1 3 5 7 9 10 8 6 4 2